WS

D0353168

70001017836 1

*For Christopher*


*The Illustrator would like to thank
the Jimmy Kennedy Estate for
allowing her to adapt the words
of The Teddy Bears' Picnic*

*First published 1998 by*
Uplands Books
1 The Uplands
Maze Hill
St Leonards
East Sussex  TN38 0HL

*Reproduced by permission of
International Music Publications*

Illustrations © 1998 Prue Theobalds

British Library Cataloguing in Publication Data
Theobalds, Prue
The teddy bears' christmas
1. Title

ISBN  1 897951 26 4 Hb
ISBN  1 897951 27 2 Pbk

The moral right of the author/illustrator has been asserted

*All rights reserved.  Without limiting the rights under copyright
reserved above, no part of this publication may be reproduced, stored in a
retrieval system or transmitted in any form or by any means, electronic,
mechanical, photocopying, or otherwise, without the prior written
permission of both the copyright owner and Uplands Books.*

# The
# Teddy Bears'
# Christmas

Pictures by
**Prue Theobalds**

*Words adapted from the lyrics of*
**The Teddy Bears' Picnic**
by Jimmy Kennedy

**UPLANDS BOOKS**

WORCESTERSHIRE COUNTY COUNCIL

836

| Morley Books | 8.10.98 |
| --- | --- |
| | £3.99 |

If you go down in the woods today
You're sure of a big surprise.

If you go down in the woods today
You'd better go in disguise;

For ev'ry bear that ever there was
Will gather there for certain, because
Today's the day the Teddy Bears have
their Christmas.

Ev'ry Teddy Bear who's been good
Is sure of a treat today.

There's lots of marvellous
things to eat,

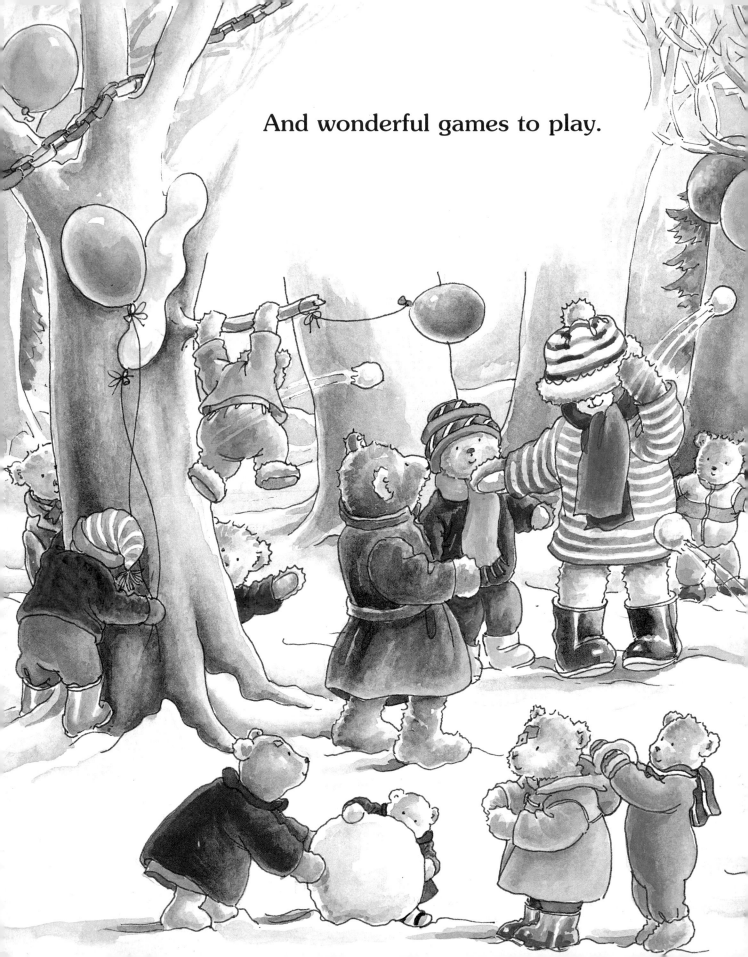

And wonderful games to play.

Beneath the trees
    where nobody sees
They'll hide and seek
    as long as they please,
'Cause that's the way
    the Teddy Bears have
    their Christmas.

If you go down in the woods today
You'd better not go alone.

It's lovely down in the woods today
But safer to stay at home.

# For ev'ry bear that ever there was

Will gather there for certain, because
Today's the day the Teddy Bears have
their Christmas.

Christmas time for Teddy Bears,

The little Teddy Bears are having a lovely time today.
Watch them, catch them unawares
And see them on their Christmas holiday.

See them gaily gad about,
They love to play and shout;
They never have any care;

At six o'clock their Mummies and Daddies
Will take them home to bed,
Because they're tired little Teddy Bears.